ALICE'S NIGHTMARE WONDERLAND

COLOURING BOOK

SNOWBOOKS

Proudly published by Snowbooks
Copyright © 2015 Jonathan Green, Kev Crossley
Jonathan Green asserts the moral right to be identified as
the author of this work.
Illustrations by Kev Crossley
All rights reserved.
Snowbooks Ltd | email: info@snowbooks.com
www.snowbooks.com.
British Library Cataloguing in Publication Data.
A catalogue record for this book is available from the
British Library.
Paperback / softback ISBN13 9781909679825
First published December 2015

Also by Jonathan Green:

Resurrection Engines Paperback / softback 9781907777844
You Are The Hero Paperback / softback 9781909679368
You Are The Hero Hardback 9781909679382
You Are The Hero Electronic book text 9781909679405
Sharkpunk Paperback / softback 9781909679962
Christmas Explained Hardback 9781909679375
Game Over Paperback / softback 9781909679573
Alice's Nightmare in Wonderland Hardback 9781909679818
Alice's Nightmare in Wonderland Electronic book text 9781909679740
Alice's Nightmare in Wonderland Paperback / softback 9781909679597

J. G. – For Clare, Jake, Mattie and Lisa

K. C. – For Fiona and Aidan

"How can I be late," Alice asks the rabbit, "when I don't even know what it is I'm late for?"

kevicrossley 2015

But as she falls, and her eyes become accustomed to the darkness, Alice realises that the sides of the well are lined with cupboards and bookshelves.

Tick-tock, tick-tock, go the clock mechanisms as the metal men stalk towards her, a sinister glint in their watch-case eyes. Tick-tock, tick-tock.

"Its name has gone down in legend as the Vorpal Sword," the Gryphon replies, "but it lies many leagues from here, on the island of the Jabberwock."

First a great twitching snout emerges from beneath the knitted shawl, followed by a set of curving yellow tusks. Cloven feet that were once an infant's hands and feet kick free of the woollen mantle as the creature shakes itself free of the blanket.

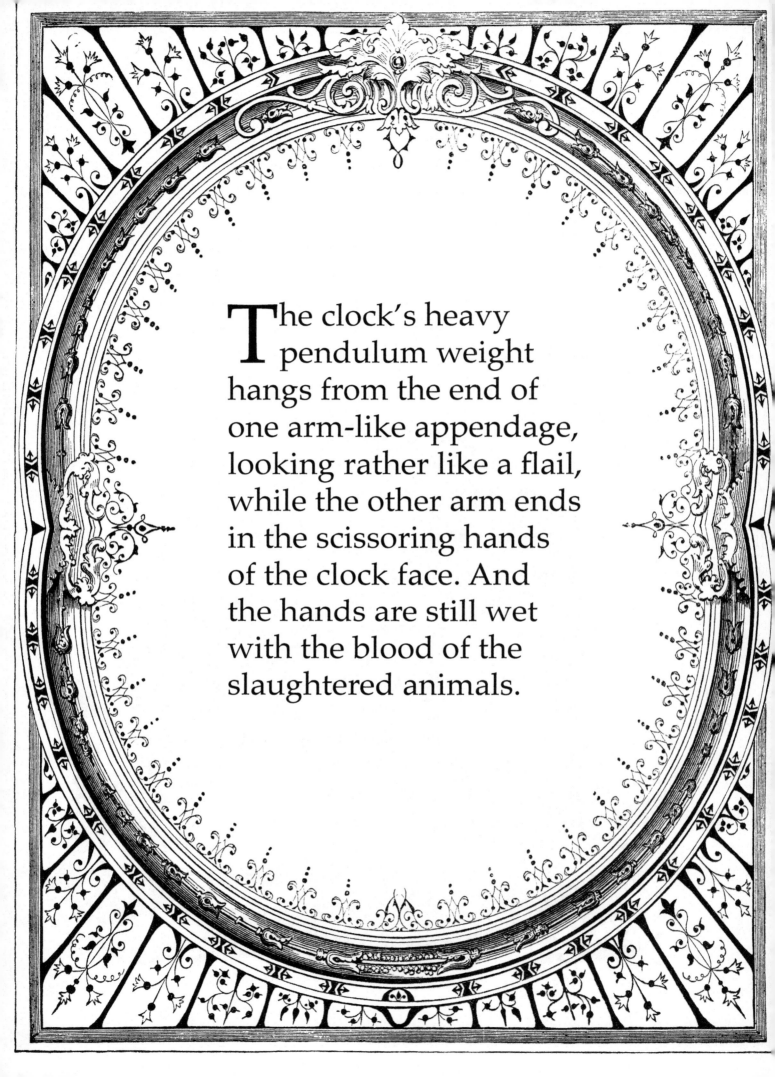

The clock's heavy pendulum weight hangs from the end of one arm-like appendage, looking rather like a flail, while the other arm ends in the scissoring hands of the clock face. And the hands are still wet with the blood of the slaughtered animals.

Alice is taken aback to find a large wooden bird, with a brass beak and gleaming metal talons, blocking her way out of the March Hare's house.

And Alice is looking up at a large mushroom, about the same height as herself; and when she has looked under it, and on both sides of it, and behind it, it occurs to her that she might as well look and see what is on the top of it.

KEV CROSSLEY 2015

"There you are," says the Cat, grinning from ear-to-ear, "I was starting to worry that we would never get the chance to speak."

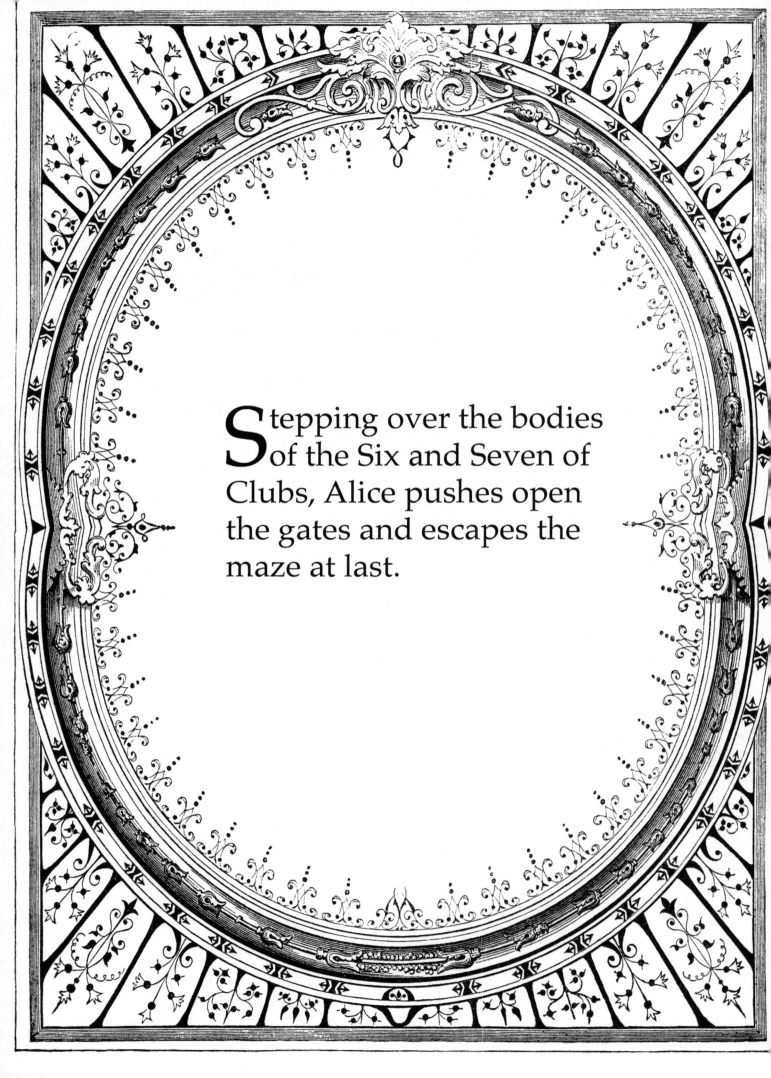

Stepping over the bodies of the Six and Seven of Clubs, Alice pushes open the gates and escapes the maze at last.

The strange creature – if it can even be called a creature – has knives and forks for fingers, and a large teapot for a head. The Tea Service stalks across the tablecloth, with rattling clattering steps, reaching for Alice with its cutlery claws.

Ignoring Alice now, the Red Knight turns to meet the ghostly White Knight's charge. Swords clash and sparks fly.

Kev Crossley 2015

Its head is a bulbous mass of soft rippling flesh, while a series of pseudopods and jointed legs run the length of both sides of its undulating body. And the thing appears to be smoking a hookah pipe.

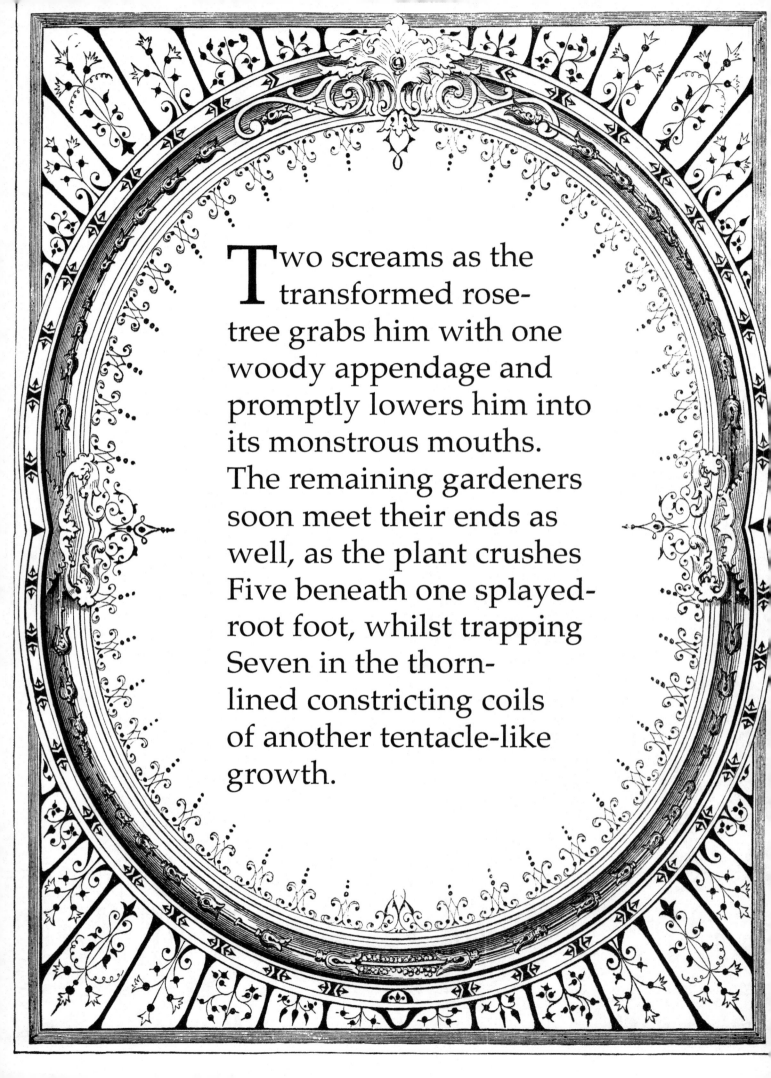

Two screams as the transformed rose-tree grabs him with one woody appendage and promptly lowers him into its monstrous mouths. The remaining gardeners soon meet their ends as well, as the plant crushes Five beneath one splayed-root foot, whilst trapping Seven in the thorn-lined constricting coils of another tentacle-like growth.

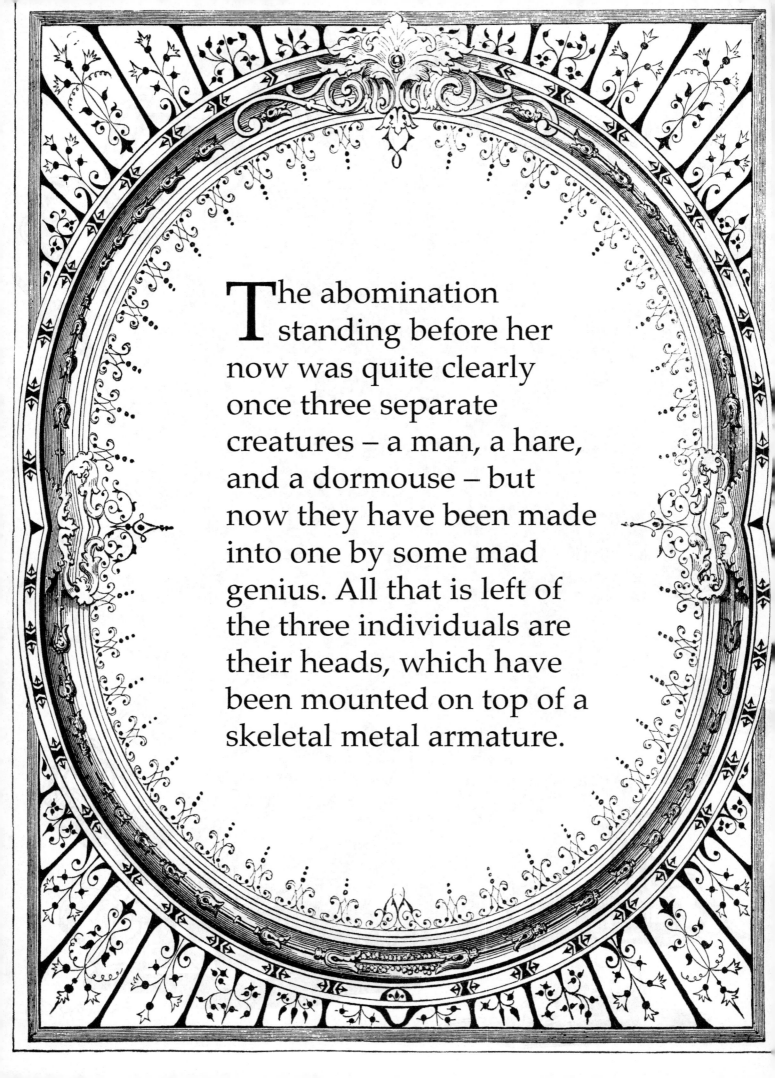

The abomination standing before her now was quite clearly once three separate creatures – a man, a hare, and a dormouse – but now they have been made into one by some mad genius. All that is left of the three individuals are their heads, which have been mounted on top of a skeletal metal armature.

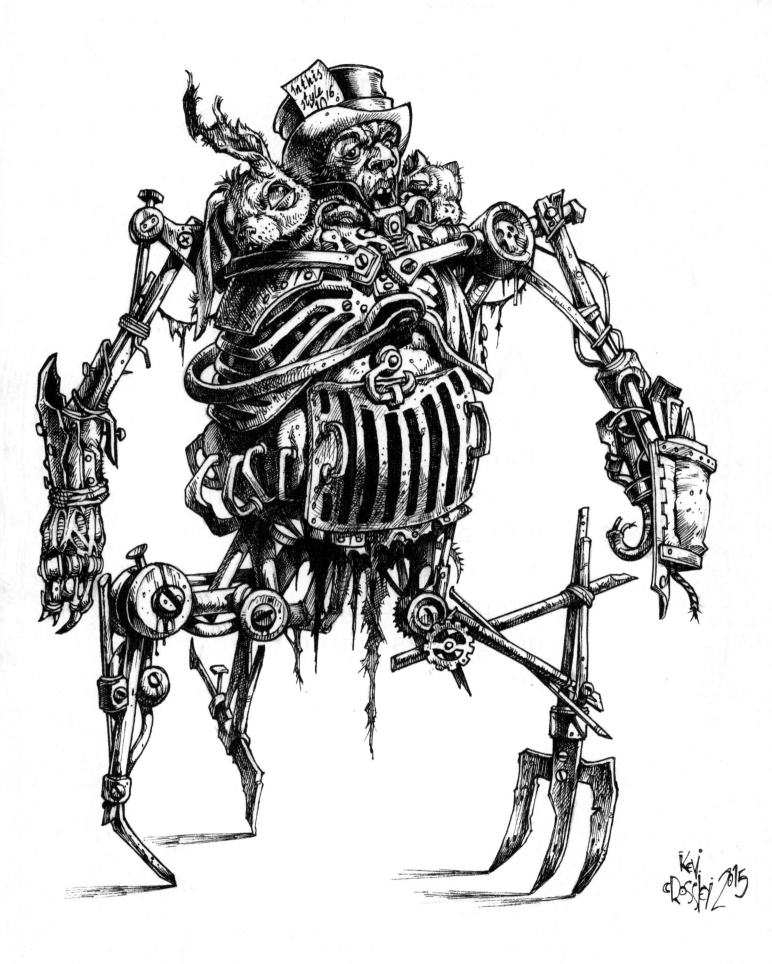

As tall as men, with a thick cloak of quills covering their backs, their fingers end in sharp claws and their eyes burn with a bestial fury. Giving a blood-curdling cry, the mutated humanoid hedgehogs bound towards her.

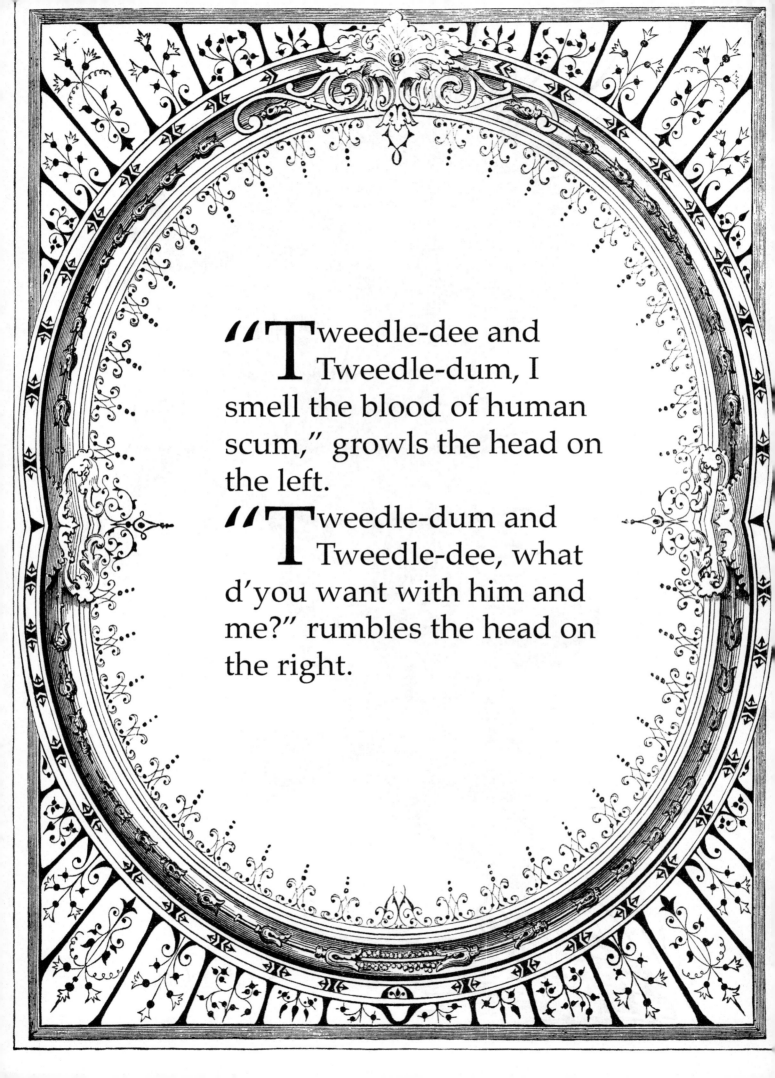

"Tweedle-dee and Tweedle-dum, I smell the blood of human scum," growls the head on the left.

"Tweedle-dum and Tweedle-dee, what d'you want with him and me?" rumbles the head on the right.

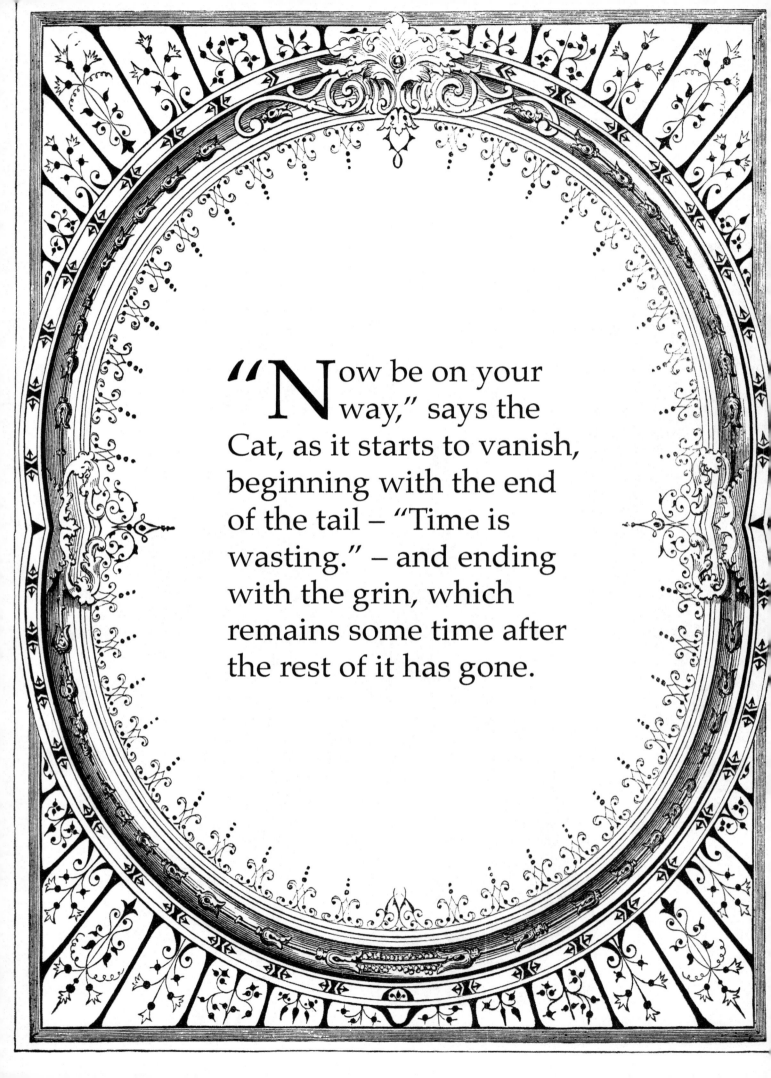

"Now be on your way," says the Cat, as it starts to vanish, beginning with the end of the tail – "Time is wasting." – and ending with the grin, which remains some time after the rest of it has gone.

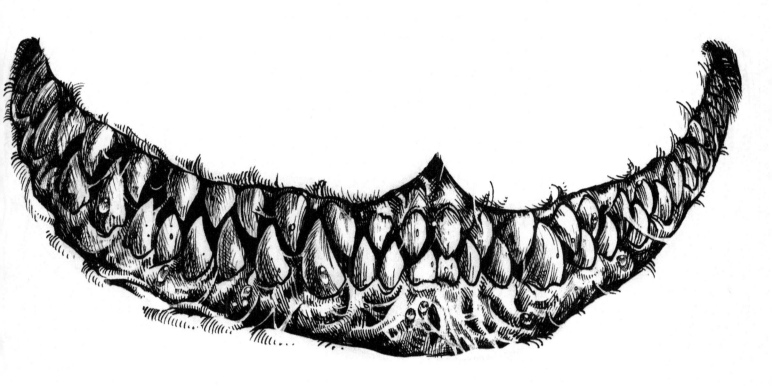

Seated upon the throne is a tall, thin woman, wearing an elegant crimson gown, its embroidered detailing making much use of a teardrop pattern, and with a delicate diadem upon her head set with a blood-red ruby.

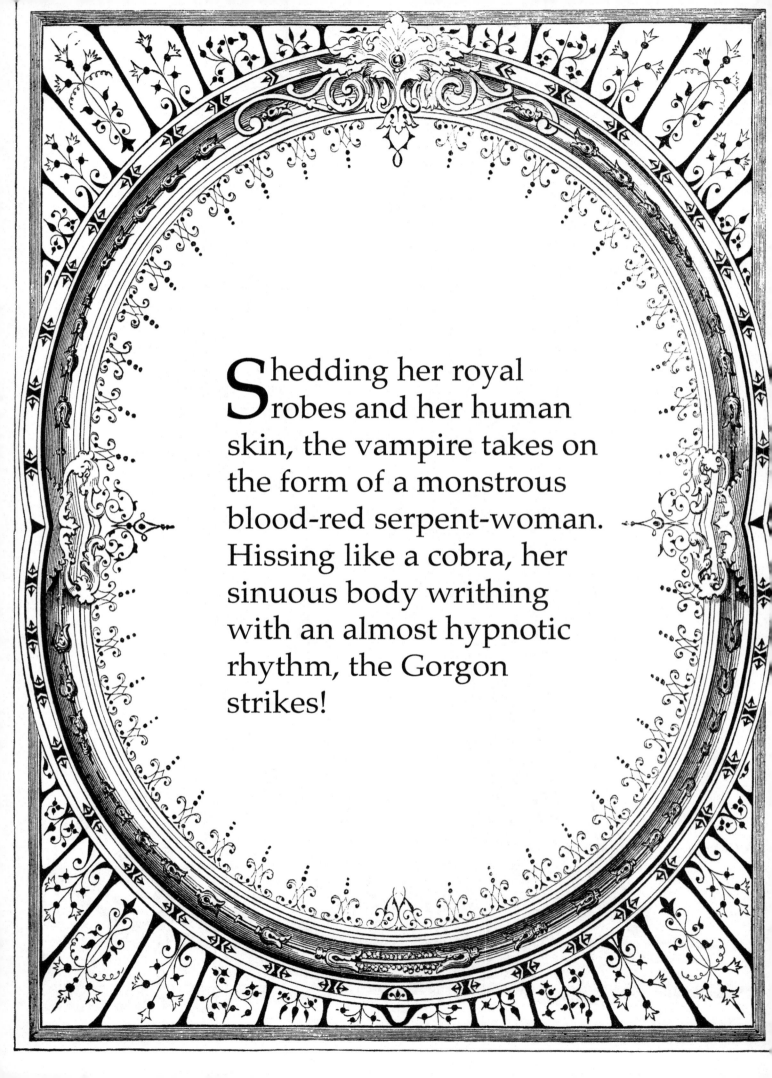

Shedding her royal robes and her human skin, the vampire takes on the form of a monstrous blood-red serpent-woman. Hissing like a cobra, her sinuous body writhing with an almost hypnotic rhythm, the Gorgon strikes!

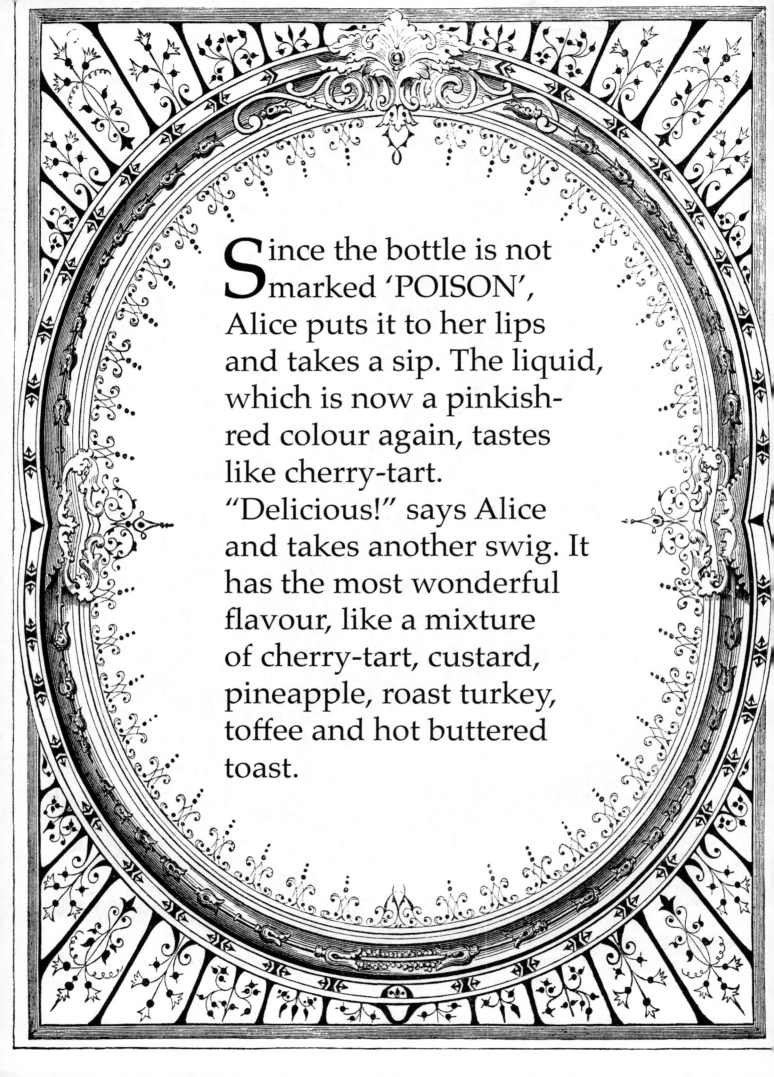

Since the bottle is not marked 'POISON', Alice puts it to her lips and takes a sip. The liquid, which is now a pinkish-red colour again, tastes like cherry-tart. "Delicious!" says Alice and takes another swig. It has the most wonderful flavour, like a mixture of cherry-tart, custard, pineapple, roast turkey, toffee and hot buttered toast.

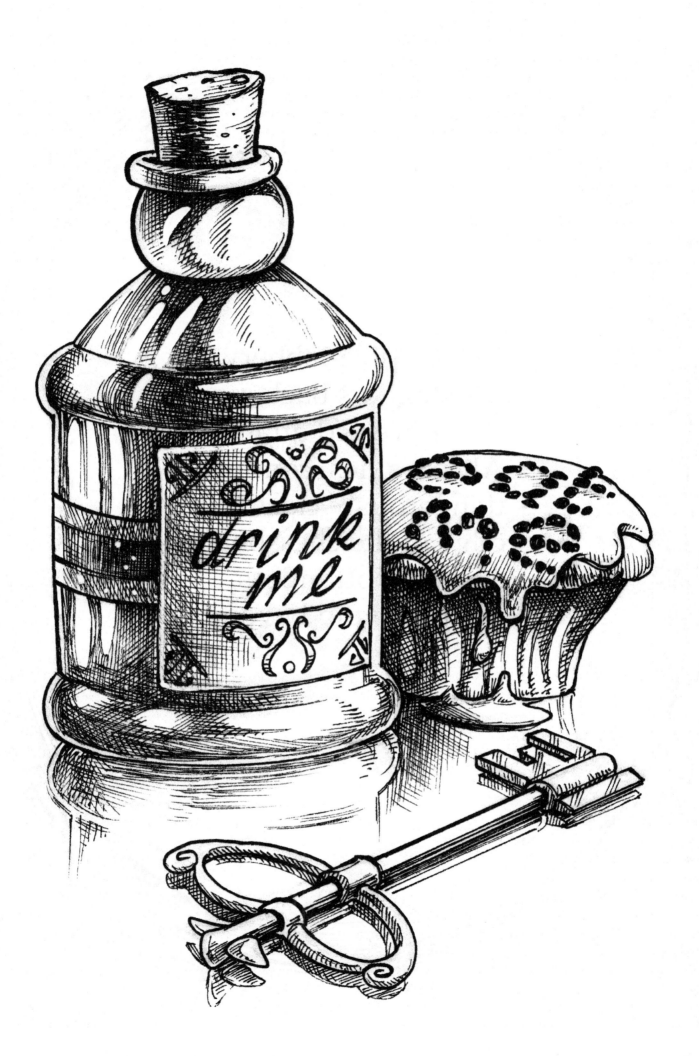

The Alice-Jabberwock staggers back, under the concerted attacks of Alice's allies, coming dangerously close to the edge of the chessboard and the bottomless, lightless void beyond.

With a leathery creak the bird turns its glass-eyed stare on the child. "Ah, Alice, it is good to see you again."

ALSO BY JONATHAN GREEN

Resurrection Engines Hardback 9781907777684
You Are The Hero Paperback / softback 9781909679368
You Are The Hero Hardback 9781909679382
You Are The Hero Electronic book text 9781909679405
Sharkpunk Paperback / softback 9781909679962
Sharkpunk Electronic book text 9781909679528
Christmas Explained Hardback 9781909679375
Game Over Electronic book text 9781909679566
Game Over Paperback / softback 9781909679573
There Leviathan Electronic book text 9781909679771

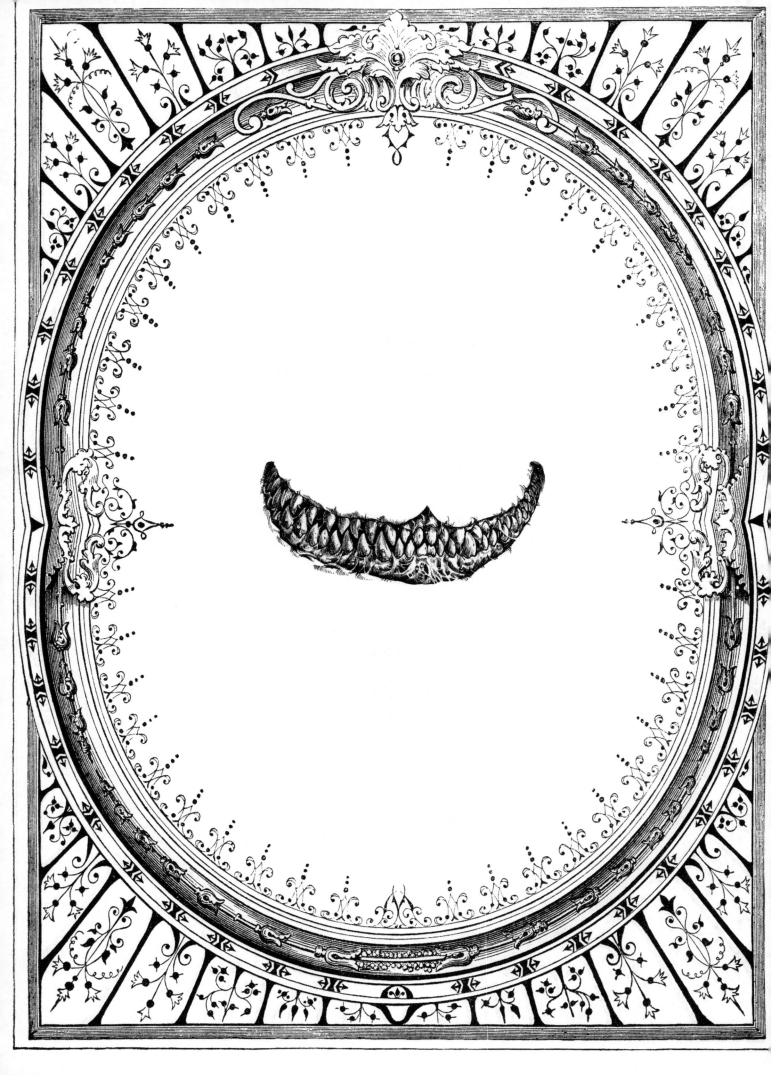

CPSIA information can be obtained
at www.ICGtesting.com
Printed in the USA
BVOW07s1447110817
491590BV00004B/36/P